A PUFFIN BOOK

PROPERTY OF

_____

_____

CATHERINE STORR was born in 1913. She was educated at St Paul's Girls' School in London and then at Newnham College, Cambridge, where she read English Literature. Although her ambition was always to be a writer, she decided to study medicine and went on to work as a psychotherapist. Catherine was married in 1942 and in 1944 had the first of her three daughters. She returned to her writing and created short stories for her young daughters, including the adventures of *Clever Polly and the Stupid Wolf*, which has remained in print ever since it was first published in 1955. Catherine wrote more than thirty much-loved books for children and young adults, which have been translated into many different languages. She died in 2001, aged eighty-seven.

Books by Catherine Storr

CATHERINE STORR

TALES OF
POLLY
AND THE HUNGRY
WOLF

Illustrated by Jill Bennett

A PUFFIN BOOK

PUFFIN BOOKS

UK | USA | Canada | Ireland | Australia
India | New Zealand | South Africa

Puffin Books is part of the Penguin Random House group of companies
whose addresses can be found at global.penguinrandomhouse.com.

puffinbooks.com

First published by Faber and Faber Limited 1980
Published in Puffin Books 1982
Reissued in this edition 2016

001

Text copyright © Catherine Storr, 1980
Illustrations copyright © Faber and Faber Limited, 1980

The moral right of the author and illustrator has been asserted

Set in 13.5/20.5 pt Sabon LT Std
Typeset by Jouve (UK), Milton Keynes
Printed in Great Britain by Clays Ltd, St Ives plc

A CIP catalogue record for this book is available from the British Library

ISBN: 978-0-141-36925-9

www.greenpenguin.co.uk

Contents

Contents

1. The Enchanted Polly

THE WOLF sat gloomily in his kitchen. Once, in happier days, he had actually had Polly there for a short time. Now all he had to comfort him was a nearly empty larder and his small library of well pawed-over books. It was one of these he was reading now.

He read about clever animals who caught beautiful little girls and kept them, sometimes as servants, sometimes as wives. Sometimes they meant to eat them. But it was disappointing that though all the tigers, lions, dragons, foxes, wolves and other animals seemed to have very little difficulty in catching their prey, most of them somehow or other failed to keep them. The beautiful little girls generally managed to escape at the last minute, often by tricks which the wolf considered very unsportsmanlike.

The story he was reading just now was about a dragon chasing a princess, who had once been in his cave, but had then run away. She couldn't run as fast as the dragon could move, but she turned herself first into a fly, then into an old woman, and lastly into a bridge over a river. The dragon never managed to recognize her in any of her disguises, and in the end he was drowned in the river under the princess-bridge.

'Terrible the things these girls get up to! No wonder I've never been able to catch that Polly. Here am I, a simple wolf, while she can turn into almost anything she chooses. It's all so unfair!' the wolf exclaimed. Then he remembered that even if he couldn't take on different shapes, he at least had brains. 'I'll show her! She shan't deceive me. Whatever she pretends to be, I shall know it's really her. I'm not stupid like that dragon. I am clever,' the wolf thought. He had heard that fish was good for the brains, so he opened a tin of tuna and gobbled it down for supper. In case that didn't do the trick, he slept with another tin of tuna under his pillow that night. He very cleverly decided not to open it first, in case the oil made a mess on the bedclothes. 'Wow! I am brilliant this evening,' he said to himself.

The next day, Polly, coming home from school, saw the wolf standing outside a shop and staring fixedly in at the window. She had hoped that he wouldn't notice her, but just as she was behind him, he turned round. She was preparing to run, when he spoke.

'Little girl!'

Polly looked around. There were plenty of people walking up and down near by, but there was no other little girl in sight.

'Little girl! Little girl!' the wolf said again.

'Are you talking to me?' Polly asked.

'Of course I am talking to you. You don't think that when I talk to myself I call myself "little girl", do you? I'm not little, for one thing, and I'm not a girl, for another. I don't make stupid mistakes like that,' the wolf said irritably.

'If you mean me, why don't you say my name?' Polly asked.

'Because I don't know it, of course. You look remarkably like a girl called Polly, but I know you aren't her because she is somewhere else, in disguise. That's why I have to call you "little girl". Now stop asking silly questions and give me a sensible answer for a change,' the wolf said.

'A sensible answer to what?'

The wolf pointed to the window he had been gazing at.

'Do you see those two flies inside the window?'

Polly looked. Sure enough, two flies were climbing up on the other side of the glass. As soon as one reached nearly to the top, it buzzed angrily down to the bottom again. The wolf was following their movements with great interest, his long tongue lolling out and sometimes twitching slightly.

'Those flies. I daresay they look just the same to you, little girl? You can't tell which is which? Can you?'

Polly looked carefully and then said, 'No, I can't.'

'You see no difference between them?'

'Perhaps that one that's crawling up now is a little bigger,' Polly said, pointing.

'Nonsense. They are exactly the same. But I'll tell you something that will surprise you. Although they look alike to you, I know which is which,' the wolf said.

'Which is which, then? I mean, if they look exactly the same, what's the difference between them?'

'You're trying to muddle me. What I mean is, I know which of them really is a proper fly and which isn't.'

'Which is the proper fly?' Polly asked.

The wolf looked closely at both flies. Then he pointed. 'That one.'

'If that's the real fly, what is the other one?' Polly asked.

'Aha! Now, little girl, you are going to be surprised. That other fly – is a girl.'

'A girl fly?'

'Don't be so stupid. Not a girl fly, a girl. A real girl, like you. A human girl. Young, plump. Well, plumpish. Delicious.'

Polly looked at the two flies again. The real fly was doing the angry buzzing act down from the top of the window to the bottom. The fly who was really a girl was skipping up the glass. At this moment she stopped and began twiddling her front pair of legs.

'You see? She knows that I know who she is. She is wringing her hands because she sees that I have penetrated her disguise and that in a moment I shall claim her as my own,' the wolf said, triumphant.

'Flies often do that with their front legs. My mother says it looks like knitting,' Polly said.

'Nonsense. Only flies that are really girls would do it. Look at the other fly. The real one.'

As the wolf said this, the other fly also stopped on its path up the window and also knitted with its front legs.

'You see?' Polly said.

'He's copying the Polly fly,' the wolf said quickly.

'Polly?' said Polly.

'That . . . Fly . . . Is . . . Only . . . Pretending to be a fly. She . . . Is . . . Really . . . A . . . Girl,' the wolf said in the loud slow tones used for speaking to fools or foreigners.

'Why?' Polly asked.

'I can't go back to the beginning. All I can tell you is that there is a maddening child who lives round here, the one who looks rather like you, called Polly. She thinks she is clever. She believes that if she disguises herself as a fly, I shan't know who she is, so she will escape from my clutches. But she's not all that clever. I don't suppose she's any cleverer than you are. And I am much too clever for her. It didn't take me any time to see that that was no ordinary fly.'

'What happens next?' Polly asked, interested.

'I catch her and eat her all up,' the wolf replied.

'I wouldn't think she'll taste very good. Not if she's still a fly.'

'She won't remain a fly. Directly I lay my paw on her and say her real name, she will be compelled to resume her ordinary shape. She'll be a girl again, like you. And then . . . Yum!' the wolf said with gusto.

'How are you going to lay your paw on her? Both those flies are inside the window and we're outside,' Polly said.

'I am now going into the shop to claim my prize,' the wolf said. He disappeared. Polly took the opportunity to get herself safely home to tea.

A day or two later, Polly, walking down the High Street, caught sight of the wolf standing very close to a group of three stout, elderly ladies, who were talking to each other as they waited for the bus. They were so busy gossiping that they didn't notice the wolf edging nearer and nearer, until he was within touching distance of the stoutest of the ladies. His paw was raised to touch the stoutest lady on the shoulder, when she turned her head and saw a very large, dark person standing uncomfortably close.

'Here! Move off, can't you? No one asked you to join the party,' she said, taking a surprised step backwards.

'Aha!' the wolf said.

'Pardon? What's that supposed to mean?' the stoutest lady asked.

'I said, Aha. You can't deceive me . . .'

'Here! Who do you think you're talking to? You be careful, me lad, or I'll get the police on to you.'

'It's no good. I know you,' the wolf said.

'I don't know you. And I don't want to, so take yourself off,' the stoutest lady said, raising her umbrella threateningly. The two women behind her pressed closer and one of them seized a handful of the wolf's fur.

'You are Polly, and I claim you as my own,' the wolf said, trying to lay a paw on the stoutest lady's shoulder.

There was a scuffle. There were cries of 'Keep your dirty paws off me!' and 'Who do you think you are?' and 'Never been so insulted in my life.' Someone was calling for the police. Others were trying to beat the wolf with sticks or umbrellas. One of the stout ladies was having hysterics. The wolf was howling with rage and pain. It was lucky for him that just then the huge red bus lumbered up, and since it was already late and the next one probably wouldn't be there for nearly an hour, the stout ladies had to leave him on the pavement, and climb into the bus, murmuring angrily as they went.

Polly felt almost sorry for the wolf. This did not prevent her from keeping a safe distance the next day, when she saw him standing disconsolately on a bridge that ran over a motorway not far from her home. He looked bedraggled. One ear had been torn, and there were small bare patches on his neck as if handfuls of fur had been pulled out. He was peering down at the motorway beneath the bridge, and Polly was wondering whether to go home and hope that he hadn't seen her, when he called out to her.

'Little girl! Little girl!'

'If he doesn't recognize me, perhaps it's safe to stay,' Polly thought, and she moved a little nearer.

'Little girl! Come and look at this bridge,' the wolf said.

'I'm looking,' Polly said.

'Have you noticed anything funny about it?' the wolf asked.

'No, I haven't. What's funny about it?' Polly called back.

'Ssssh. Don't shout like that. She might hear.'

'Who might hear?'

'Polly.'

'Where is Polly?' Polly asked. She wanted to see just how stupid the wolf could be.

'She has turned herself into a bridge this time,' the wolf said.

'A bridge? Why?'

'You must be the same little girl who was so stupid last time I tried to explain about Polly. She turns herself into different shapes so that I shan't recognize her. Don't you remember? Last time she was disguised as an old lady. The time before that she was a fly. This time it's a bridge. In the stories it's a bridge over a river, but there doesn't seem to be a river round here, so I suppose she thought a motorway would do instead. She's made one mistake, though.'

'What's that?' Polly asked.

'This bridge hasn't got a road going over it. And it's got steps each end. That's stupid. How can cars climb up steps?'

'This bridge isn't meant for cars. It's meant for people,' Polly said.

'Nonsense. Bridges are meant for cars. And horses and carts. Why should there be a bridge just for people? They can walk across a bridge for cars, but cars can't climb stairs and get across a silly bridge like this. That's how I know it isn't a real bridge. It's that stupid little Polly,' the wolf said.

'So what are you going to do?' Polly asked.

'I shall seize her and tell her that I know that it's her. Then she has to go back to her real shape. Then I shall eat her,' the wolf said.

'That's what you said before,' Polly said.

'When? What did I say before? Something very intelligent, I'm sure.'

'When you were watching those flies. What happened to them?'

'The flies. Oh, that,' the wolf said.

'Yes, that. Wasn't one of the flies Polly after all?'

'Of course it was. I told you so at the time,' the wolf said.

'Then why didn't you catch her and eat her up?' Polly asked.

'It was very confusing. They buzzed so. And rushed up and down the window. You saw for yourself. They were very much alike, you must agree.'

'I couldn't tell which was which,' Polly said.

'Exactly. That was the difficulty,' the wolf said.

'So you got the wrong one?'

'I laid my paw on the Polly fly and said her name. Nothing happened. I had got the real fly by mistake. Meanwhile the other fly, the Polly fly, had gone. Flown. It was most disappointing.'

'What went wrong with the old ladies?' Polly asked.

The wolf looked surprised and pained.

'It was a disgraceful affair. I should prefer not to talk about it. I was treated abominably.'

'And now you've discovered that Polly is disguised as this bridge?' Polly asked.

'That's right.'

'What are you waiting for? When are you going to lay your hand on this bridge and say that you know who it really is?' Polly asked. She was ready to run if she thought the wolf might come to his senses and make a grab for the real Polly.

'I'm just making sure in my mind that I remember how to swim,' the wolf said.

'What has swimming got to do with it?' Polly asked, surprised.

The wolf groaned loudly.

'I must say that for sheer stupidity you beat even that stupid little Polly I was telling you about. Don't you ever read a good book? Don't you know that the princess turns herself into a bridge, and the dragon or the giant or the wolf who is after her stands on the bridge and says her real name and then she turns back into a princess again? And then the dragon, or whoever it is, falls into the river below and is drowned. That's because dragons are stupid. But I am not stupid. I have very cleverly had swimming lessons in the public baths. I just have to remember how to work my front and back legs, and I shan't drown. Instead I shall quickly swim to the river bank, climb out and eat up the princess. I mean, I shall eat up the Polly.'

'But there isn't a river under this bridge,' Polly pointed out.

The wolf looked down at the endless procession of lorries, cars and coaches passing beneath the bridge.

'No. I had forgotten. In that case there's no need to wait. I don't have to remember how to swim and I needn't get my fur wet. So much the better.' He turned towards the middle of the bridge.

'Wolf!' Polly called after him.

'What is it now?'

'When you say Polly's name and the bridge disappears, you won't be in a river, but you will be down there,' Polly said, pointing down to the motorway.

'What about it?' the wolf said.

'The traffic won't stop for you. All the cars and coaches and things are going much too fast. Their brakes couldn't work quickly enough. You'll get run over. Squashed. Flat as a pancake,' Polly said.

The wolf stopped. He looked over the railing to the stream of traffic below.

'Are you quite sure they won't stop?' he asked.

'Quite sure.'

'You wouldn't like to do a small scientific experiment? You jump down there and we shall see how many cars stop and what happens to you?'

'No, thank you, Wolf. I wouldn't like to do that at all,' said clever Polly.

The wolf returned from the middle of the bridge and stood carefully to one side.

'Do you think I should be safe if I fell from here?' he asked.

'It's still quite a long way to fall on to the ground,' Polly said.

'What would you suggest then?'

'I think you should go over to the other side. Then you should go down the steps to the bottom, so that you don't fall anywhere. Then you can lay your paw on that end of the bridge and tell it that you know it's Polly,' Polly said.

'You are really quite a kind little girl. And not as much stupider than Polly as I thought,' the wolf said, preparing to do as Polly had advised. Halfway across the bridge he turned and looked back.

'Wait there and see the great transformation! See a bridge turn into a Polly and get snapped up by the clever wolf,' he shouted.

But Polly knew better than that. Before the wolf had got down the steps on the further side of the motorway, Polly had run home. She didn't want to risk being chased and caught, when the wolf discovered that the bridge was only a bridge after all.

2. The Great Eating Competition

'I DARE you!' the wolf said loudly. He had to speak loudly, because he and Polly had met in the High Street on a Saturday morning, and there were plenty of other noises, over which he wanted to make himself heard. Cars were grinding up the hill, horns were blowing, motorbikes were revving, children were calling, babies were yelling and people were shouting so that their friends could hear what they were saying.

'What do you dare me to do?' Polly shouted back.

'A trial of strength. A trial of something or other. You know the sort of thing. We could try which of us could lift the heaviest stone.'

'There aren't any heavy stones around here,' Polly said, looking up and down the High Street.

'We could try that lady. I'm sure she weighs as much as a really large stone.' The wolf pointed a paw towards a very large lady, just about to go over a zebra crossing.

'I wouldn't try to lift her, if I were you. If you did, she'd probably call the police and have you put in prison.' Polly wasn't sure whether or not the wolf might have been able to lift the lady, but she was quite sure that she herself would not be able to.

'Oh, all right. You suggest something, then,' the wolf said, sulkily.

'Shall we see who can talk the fastest?' Polly asked.

'That's mean! You know you'd win that. Not because I haven't got plenty to say, and very well worth saying too. But because I like to think before I speak.'

'I've read a story where the people tried to see who could tell the biggest lie,' Polly said.

'I am shocked. I am horrified. I thought you were a good, truth-telling girl,' the wolf said primly. He spoiled the effect by asking quickly, 'What did they say? What was the biggest lie?'

'I meant a made-up story. Like someone saying he'd taken a bite out of the moon,' Polly said.

'Really? That would explain a lot. I have often wondered why the moon so often seems to have suffered from some sort of attack. Sometimes from one side, sometimes from the other. Often you can see just where someone has taken a bite out of her. I never knew that before,' the wolf said, considering the matter.

'But I didn't mean that that was true. I meant, that was the sort of story someone might make up.'

'But why should he say so if it isn't true?'

'To see if anyone else could think of a bigger lie,' Polly said.

'Easy! Anything would be a bigger lie than saying that there is someone taking bites out of the moon. You can see that it's true every now and then, by just looking at her.'

Polly felt unable to go on with the subject. It was obviously not going to be possible to convince the wolf that someone was not regularly taking mouthfuls of moon. She waited for his next remark.

'I'll tell you what. Suppose we have a competition to see which of us could eat up the other one fastest,' the wolf said.

Polly thought about this. She was puzzled. 'How would that work?' she asked.

'Simple. Simple to anyone with any brains, that is. Suppose I start eating you at, say, ten o'clock this morning . . .'

Polly looked at the clock tower. The clock showed that it was now a quarter to ten.

'We have an umpire, with a watch. I eat as fast as I can, and when I have finished, snap, gobble-you-up, crackle, crunch, I tell him so. He looks around to make sure that there's nothing left that could reasonably be considered eatable. I shouldn't be eating your clothes, you know, Polly. I should kindly leave them for you or another little girl to use again.'

'But they wouldn't be much use to me if you'd eaten me all up,' Polly pointed out.

The wolf took no notice of this and hurried on. 'So, I tell the umpire. He looks at his watch and he sees that I have taken exactly forty minutes. Fifty perhaps. It would depend on how tough you had turned out to be, and on other details which I won't mention just now. Then the umpire announces that I have won. Easy!' The wolf sounded very much pleased with himself.

'What happens when it's my turn to eat you up?' Polly asked.

'It would take you far longer than forty or fifty minutes to eat me. It might take you hours. Possibly even a whole day. I am larger than you. I am exceedingly tough. And then there's the hair,' the wolf said.

'What about hair?'

'Hair is a great slower-down of fast eating. Hair in the wrong places can make a quick snap almost impossible. I mean in the wrong places for a mouthful, of course. Naturally for a wolf it is right and proper to have hair all over. A great deal of hair, covering most of his body. While you are very nearly quite bald. Your hair all grows in one place, on top of your face. It would be easy to get rid of it in five minutes or so, while it would take you several hours to get rid of mine, I reckon,' the wolf said with pride.

'But if it had been me that started, you wouldn't have had a chance to try. I would have eaten you first.'

'That's why I should start. After all, as we know that I could eat you faster than you could eat me, there wouldn't be any point in your trying.'

'But that wouldn't be fair!' Polly exclaimed.

'Life is not fair. Some people are born as wolves, others are only feeble little girls. Some people are born with brains. Others are stupid from the beginning. There's nothing you can do about that.'

'You can do something about trying to make a competition fair,' Polly said.

'What do you mean? You couldn't make yourself eat twice as fast, could you? Only it would have to be more like a hundred times as fast.'

'I don't think anyone could make me eat that much faster. But they could make you eat more slowly. That's what they do when there is a horse-race,' Polly said.

'Do you have races where horses eat each other? I never knew. I'd like to see that.'

'Don't be disgusting, Wolf. They don't eat each other. They gallop. The horse that gallops fastest wins the race. If one horse is much faster than the others, it has to carry a heavier weight than the others. They fasten pieces of lead to its saddle, to slow it down,' Polly said.

'How monstrous! Poor horse. Terribly unfair.'

'No, it isn't. It makes the race fairer for the other horses. The slower ones have a chance to win.'

'Now, let's stop thinking about boring things like galloping horses. Let's talk about us,' the wolf suggested.

'Don't you see? If we are going to have an eating race, we have to make it as fair as we can, by making you eat more slowly.'

'I can assure you, Polly, that no amount of heavy weights on my saddle would make any difference to my eating habits. And anyway, I don't have a saddle. So you will find it all very difficult. Probably quite impossible,' the wolf said. He moved a little nearer to Polly and a long red tongue came out and licked his wicked lips.

'Of course it wouldn't be any good putting weights on you. No one wants to stop you from running fast,' Polly said.

'Right! So what are we waiting for?'

'We have to think of something that stops you eating so fast.'

'I should like to see what could do that,' the wolf said.

'We could put a sort of clamp into your mouth so that you couldn't open it very wide.'

'Not wide enough to take a large bite out of a juicy little Polly?' the wolf asked.

'That's right. You'd only be able to take a tiny bite at a time.'

'That wouldn't be any fun. If you can't take a really large, refreshing bite out of something you fancy, half the pleasure of eating goes,' the wolf complained.

'Perhaps a muzzle would be better. You see dogs wearing them over their noses sometimes.'

'Then I wouldn't be able to eat at all.'

'You'd probably be able to drink,' Polly said kindly.

'While you were crunching away at me? That would be terrible.'

'Or perhaps . . . ? Yes. I think probably that's what they'd do. That would be much the best way,' Polly said, looking at the wolf's large mouth full of teeth.

'What?' the wolf asked, trembling slightly.

'We could fix your teeth.'

'What do you mean by fix?'

'Make them blunt. File them, so that they aren't sharp enough to bite quickly,' Polly said.

'File my beautiful, long, sharp teeth!'

'No. Now I think about it, that would take too long. It would be easier to take most of them out,' Polly said.

'Take them out!' the wolf repeated. He seemed dazed.

'We wouldn't take out the front ones. We don't want to spoil your looks. Just the back teeth,' Polly explained.

'But it's the teeth at the back that do half the work. The grinding up of the meat, the crunching of the bones . . .'

'That's why they'd have to come out. I daresay they'd try to do it without hurting you too much. Sometimes they make people go to sleep before they pull out a really big tooth,' Polly said kindly.

'All my teeth are big,' the wolf said.

'I can see that. So you could ask the dentist to give you gas and air, and then you'd go to sleep and he could take them all out at once.'

The wolf shivered.

'It would be a long time before they grew again,' he said.

'I don't think they would grow again. You're too old. It's only very young creatures who grow a second set of teeth when the first ones come out.'

The wolf ran his tongue over his teeth, counting them fondly.

'I could promise to eat very slowly,' he said.

'You might forget in the excitement of getting me to eat at last.'

'I could drink a glass of water between each mouthful.'

'Very bad for the digestion. You don't want to ruin your stomach so that you'd never enjoy another meal,' Polly said.

'Would they be taking out your teeth too?' the wolf asked.

Polly shook her head. 'They wouldn't need to. Even with all my teeth, I wouldn't be able to eat faster than you,' she said.

The wolf considered this.

'Polly!'

'Yes, Wolf?'

'It was a good idea of yours that we should try which of us could eat the other fastest, but now that I have thought the matter over carefully I think it might not work very well. I feel that the end result might not be quite what we expected. I think we had better forget the whole plan.'

'I understand,' Polly said.

'I am sorry to have to disappoint you. The fact is that today I happen to be very busy. I have a great many things to attend to at home. Also I happen not to be particularly hungry this morning. I believe that all I shall be able to manage for my dinner will be a lightly boiled egg. Perhaps also a small piece of dry toast. I don't really feel equal to tackling a whole Polly just now.'

'That's quite all right. I don't really want to eat you today, Wolf,' Polly said politely.

'Another time,' the wolf called as he turned down the High Street towards his home. As he trotted off he was congratulating himself on his great cleverness. He had quickly seen the dangers into which Polly had tried to entrap him. The horror of having his jaws clamped together! The shame of wearing a muzzle like a dog! Worse still, the loss of any of his useful, long, sharp (and rather yellow) teeth!

'Foiled again! Who says I am not the cleverest? As well, of course, as much the quickest eater,' the wolf murmured to himself. It was only a pity, he thought, that he hadn't had the chance to prove it this time.

3. The Spell

THE WOLF shut his large book with a loud bang.

'Of course! What I need is a spell! A spell which would make that stupid little Polly come to see me, asking me to be kind enough to eat her up,' he said.

He was amazed that the idea hadn't occurred to him before. In the book he had just been reading there was no shortage of spells. Beautiful princesses got turned into frogs, frogs turned into handsome princes, kings were trapped and enchanted by witches, several small juicy children were forced, by magic, to work for giants and ogres or other unpleasant characters and were often in the gravest danger of being eaten. If all this could happen to princesses and princes, why shouldn't a perfectly ordinary little Polly be made, by a spell, to come and look for a very respectable wolf? And even made to ask him to eat her? Without any fuss, and without any of this endless argument. The wolf was bored with argument. All he wanted was a good meal, and to know that at last he had got the better of Polly, clever as she was supposed to be.

He thought carefully. He had to find a really reliable spell. He didn't want one which was going to run out at an awkward moment. Or one which never got going. The wolf put some money into a small leather bag which he tied securely round his neck, and trotted off to see what the High Street shops had to offer.

A shop window piled with saucepans, pails, baskets, cat litter and bottles of different-coloured mixtures first attracted him. A solid-looking stool was labelled 'Built to last'. This sounded promising. The wolf didn't want a long-lasting stool, of course, but if this shop sold reliable stools, why not surefire spells? He was encouraged by seeing that a bottle of purplish liquid was apparently called MAGICLEAN. He went boldly into the shop.

'I want a spell,' the wolf said to a stupid-looking girl who was leaning against a white kitchen cupboard and reading a newspaper.

'A what?'

'A spell.'

'Don't keep them. No one asks for them nowadays,' the girl said, without taking her eyes from the page in front of her.

'Yes, you do. I saw one in the window.'

'Must have made a mistake. Told you, we don't keep them. They're out of date,' the girl said, still not looking at the wolf.

'I tell you, I saw it. Here. Look!' the wolf said, seeing more bottles of the same purplish stuff on a shelf near by.

'What, that? Why didn't you say so?' the girl said. She snatched a bottle from the shelf, and began searching in a drawer for a paper bag.

'That'll be seventy-nine pence,' she said.

'Wait a moment. What does it do?' the wolf asked.

'What do you mean, what does it do?'

'What I say. What does the magic do? It might not be what I need. What I want is a simple spell which will make a small girl . . .'

'I don't know what you're on about. Can't you read? This is for cleaning out ovens. Says so on the label,' the girl said. She put the bottle within an inch or two of the wolf's nose. The printing on the label was very small and the wolf was unable to read a word.

'Is that all? Just cleans ovens? Nothing else?' he said, disappointed.

'What d'you expect for seventy-nine p? A beauty cream? Though it would take more than that to make you fit to look at,' the girl said unpleasantly. She put the bottle back on its shelf and returned to her newspaper. The wolf, insulted, went quickly out of the shop.

'What a very disagreeable girl. And stupid! Even stupider than Polly,' he thought. He stopped in front of another shop window to examine his own reflection.

'I don't know what she can have meant by that remark about a beauty cream. I am a remarkably good-looking wolf,' he decided, and, slightly comforted by what he had seen, went on his way.

He stopped next to visit a food store. He found it difficult to pass by the containers of frozen meat, though he knew from past experience that you had to wait for hours before you could get your teeth properly into those tempting-looking hunks. He passed the shelves of bread and biscuits. At last he found what he was looking for. A small packet. On the outside was printed 'TENDERIZER. FOR ANY KIND OF MEAT.'

He carried three packets to the check-out desk.

'Does it really work?' he asked the girl who rang up the cost on the cash register.

'Like magic,' she said.

'Have you got any more magic spells?' the wolf asked, interested. But by this time the girl was attending to the customer behind

the wolf, and she took no notice of his question, only pushed his three packets of tenderizer towards him.

Outside the shop, the wolf looked carefully at the instructions on the packets. 'SPRINKLE A FEW DROPS ON THE MEAT BEFORE COOKING. LEAVE FOR TEN TO FIFTEEN MINUTES BEFORE PUTTING IN THE OVEN,' he read. He opened the packet. Inside was a small bottle.

Very carefully the wolf sprinkled three or four drops on to his own front leg.

'If it makes me tender, it really is magic,' he thought.

He stood still on the pavement, watching the clock on the clock tower. At the end of ten minutes, he opened his mouth and brought his front leg towards it.

'Wow! That hurt!' he said in surprise as his teeth met his own skin. He looked quickly round. He would not have liked Polly to see him testing his own tenderness in this way.

She might have thought it was stu ... not a very clever thing to do.

He continued to walk down the street, looking in all the windows as he went. Presently he stopped outside a shop called simply HEALTH. In the window were two pictures. One was of a miserable-looking woman with a great many wrinkles, bags under her eyes and hair like string. The other showed the same woman, but this time smiling, with a smooth skin and shining hair. In her hand she held a box of globules to which she was pointing. Under the picture were the words, 'Magical transformation. I grew ten years younger in a single night.'

'That is something like magic!' the wolf thought admiringly, and he pushed open the shop door and went straight in.

'I see you have boxes of magic pills. What I want is a spell . . .' he began saying to the anxious-looking woman behind the counter.

'A smell? Ah, yes. Can I suggest these charming little lavender bags . . . so delicious. You can just sprinkle them about your linen cupboard . . .' she began.

'No, you don't understand. I want a magic potion. Something you drink. Or eat. I'll have a couple of those boxes of globules the lady in the window has in her hand,' the wolf said. Making Polly younger when he caught her would also make her tenderer and possibly stupider. While the worried woman was finding the pills, the wolf wandered round the shop. The more he looked, the more sure he became that this was the right place for spells. So many bottles full of different-coloured fluids! So many small packages done up with gold string, with pictures of herbs outside. When the wolf caught sight of a black cat stalking through the shop, and then saw an old-fashioned twig broom leaning in a corner, he knew he had at last found a witch's lair.

'That's her broom, I suppose,' he said to the worried woman.

'The besom, yes. We like the old customs here,' she said, making a neat parcel out of the two boxes of pills.

'Do you use it too? I suppose it's strong enough,' the wolf said. The woman looked as if she'd be quite a load.

'I find it far better than any of the modern brooms,' the woman said. 'Can I interest you in anything else?' she asked.

'I'd be very much interested in anything that could make a young girl behave kindly to wol . . . to animals,' the wolf said.

'Do you mean she isn't kind to our dumb friends?' the woman asked, shocked.

'She certainly isn't.'

'Treats them badly? Pulls the wings off flies? Doesn't look after her pets?'

'Starves them,' the wolf said sadly.

'But that's terrible!'

'Haven't you got something which would change her? A bottle of medicine? Some more pills?'

The anxious woman shook her head. 'Nothing will change a bad nature like that except education. Someone must take her in hand and teach her. What a terrible story! Perhaps you could give her little lessons and tell her how wickedly she's behaving?'

'I've been trying for years. But it's a very difficult case,' the wolf said sadly. He picked up his parcel and left the shop.

A day or two later, Polly was upstairs in her bedroom when she heard a loud knock on the front door. She thought of going down to see who it was, but she had learned to be careful, so she opened the window and looked cautiously out to see who was below. There was nothing and no one to be seen.

She went downstairs and saw a small parcel lying on the doormat inside the front door. A label tied on it said simply TO POLLY.

'A present. But it isn't my birthday,' Polly thought. She sat down on the mat and tore off the paper.

Inside was a round pill-box. The piece of paper stuck to the lid had writing on it, which read:

MAGIC!

UNTIL YOU TRY THIS MAGIC REMEDY

YOU WILL NEVER BELIEVE HOW

THE WRINKLES WILL FADE AWAY

THE SKIN BECOMES CLEAR AND

YOUTHFUL

YOUR STEP REGAINS ITS SPRING

LIFE LOOKS PROMISING

MAKES YOU TEN YEARS YOUNGER.

TAKE THREE GLOBULES AFTER

EACH MEAL

The pill-box was full of large green globules.

As Polly was looking at them, she heard the letter box rattle and the end of a long black nose pushed itself a short way through.

'Am oom om em?' a muffled voice asked.

'I don't understand,' Polly said.

'Bother. Can't talk with that trap thing round my mouth. I said, "Have you got them?"' the wolf's ordinary voice said from the other side of the door.

'The green globules?' Polly asked.

'From a friend,' said the voice.

'What am I supposed to do with them?'

'Swallow them, of course. How can anyone be quite so stupid?' the voice said, impatient.

'But it says on the box that they will take away my wrinkles, and I haven't got any,' Polly said.

'Perhaps the globules will prevent your getting any.'

'And they are supposed to make my skin clear and my step springy.'

'Well? You don't want to have muddy skin and to plod around like a camel, do you?' the wolf asked.

'And, Wolf! It says the globules will make me ten years younger,' Polly called out.

'And that much tenderer. A delicate morsel. Like one of those very small sucking pigs you see sometimes in butchers' shops. A very small Polly . . .' The wolf's voice died away into happy dreams of guzzling greed.

'But . . .'

'Don't let's have any of this endless talk, girl. Eat up your nice globules and don't argue,' the wolf said.

'But, Wolf, you haven't counted. The globules will make me ten years younger.'

'Hurry up and swallow them, then. I'm hungry.'

'Wolf, I am seven years old,' Polly said.

'Seven. Eight. Six. What does it matter now?'

'You aren't very good at numbers, Wolf. I am seven. If I eat these globules, and they make me ten years younger, how old do you think I shall be?'

'Two? One and a half? Six months? All good ages. Delicious ages. Just what I enjoy most,' the wolf said.

'You can't count, Wolf. If you take ten away from seven, it leaves minus three.'

'What is minus?' the wolf's voice asked suspiciously.

'It would mean that I wouldn't get born for another three years.'

'Say that again. Slowly,' the voice said.

'If . . . I . . . eat . . . these globules and they make me . . . ten . . . years . . . younger . . . I shan't get born again as a baby for another . . . three . . . years.'

There was a short silence.

'Are you sure of that?' the voice asked.

'Numbers is my best subject at school,' Polly said.

'Another three years, you said. You mean that there wouldn't be any Polly for that long? I'd have to wait for three whole years?'

'That's right,' Polly said.

'And then you would get born? A small, fat, juicy Polly? Who wouldn't have learned to talk? No, it's no good. I can't wait that long,' the wolf's voice said from the other side of the door. Polly heard a disappointed groan.

'Do you want me to start straight away?' Polly called out. There was no answer. Polly peeped through the letter box and saw a dejected-looking tail disappearing towards the garden gate. A second box of green globules flew off to one side of the owner of the tail. On the other side went a small bottle of tenderizer. 'Spells. You can't trust them now like you could in the good old days,' the wolf muttered angrily as, once more disappointed, he trotted towards his own home.

4. Songs My Mother Taught Me

IT WAS early evening and just beginning to
get dark. A huge yellow moon was hanging
about behind the trees, three times as large as
necessary. Polly was sitting on the window-
seat, practising the recorder. She hadn't
been learning very long, and she could only
play easy tunes. 'Baa, Baa, Black Sheep'
wasn't too bad. 'I Had a Little Nut Tree' was
better.

By the time she'd played it through six
times, her mouth and her fingers were tired.
She put the recorder down and looked out of

the window. It didn't really surprise her to see the wolf standing beyond the hedge, making signs at her.

Polly opened the window a little. She was on the first floor and she felt safe up there.

'Hi, Wolf!' she said.

'Did you hear that?' the wolf asked.

'Did I hear what?' Polly said.

'That horrible noise. That caterwauling. As if a grasshopper were trying to sing with his hind legs . . .'

'That was me practising my recorder,' Polly said, offended.

'You mean you meant to make that noise? Did it on purpose?'

'I didn't think I was that bad. "I Had a Little Nut Tree" was all right.'

'Do you really think so? I've always thought it a very disappointing song,' the wolf said.

'Disappointing? Because it didn't have any nuts? I'd rather have the silver nutmeg and the golden pear.'

The wolf looked astonished. 'I don't know what you're talking about,' he said.

Polly recited:

> *'I had a little nut tree*
> *Nothing would it bear,*
> *But a silver nutmeg*
> *And a golden pear.*
> *The King of Spain's daughter . . .'*

'Nonsense! You've got it entirely wrong. It's not at all like that,' the wolf said, testily.

'No, I haven't. I learned it at school,' Polly said.

'I learned it from my mother. This is what she taught me:

> *I had a little nut tree*
> *That wasn't any good.*
> *I really wanted meat, but*
> *It had only wood,'*

said the wolf.

'Trees never do have meat,' Polly said.

'Then why sing about them?'

'I don't, much. It's just that it's not so difficult to play,' Polly said.

'You call that playing? What other songs do you know?'

'Humpty Dumpty,' Polly said.

'Go on, then. No, not on that revolting penny whistle . . .'

'It's not a penny whistle. It's my new recorder,' Polly protested.

'Whatever it is, leave it alone. Just tell me the words,' the wolf said.

Polly began:

'Humpty Dumpty sat on a wall,
Humpty Dumpty had a great fall.
All the King's horses and all the King's men
Couldn't put Humpty Dumpty together again.'

'Wrong,' the wolf sighed.

'What do you mean, wrong?' Polly asked.

'You've never learned the right words. Listen:

Humpty Dumpty sat on a wall,
Humpty Dumpty had a great fall.
I licked up the yolk and the white as well,
But I couldn't be bothered with the shell,'

said the wolf.

'You ate him!' Polly said, shocked.

The wolf looked slightly ashamed. Then he said, 'Well, if the King's men couldn't help the poor old fat thing, there wasn't much I could do, was there?'

Polly thought about this.

'You eat eggs, don't you? He was only a great big egg,' the wolf said.

'Ye . . . es. Only not raw,' Polly said.

'Raw eggs are very good for the voice,' the wolf said. He opened his jaws widely and yodelled. Then he sang:

'Mary had a little lamb . . .'

'I know that. And it's not about eating,' Polly said, pleased.

'What do you mean it's not about eating? It's not about anything else,' the wolf said.

> *'Mary had a little lamb,*
> *Its fleece was white as snow,*
> *And everywhere that Mary went*
> *The lamb was sure to go,'*

Polly said.

'No,' the wolf cried, outraged.

'Yes. That's what it says,' Polly said.

'Of course it doesn't. Who wants to know about the colour of its fleece? What my mother taught me is far more interesting,' the wolf said, and raising a paw in the air, he declaimed:

> *'Mary had a little lamb,*
> *And then, not feeling full,*

58

She had some more, and more, until
All that was left was wool.

And who cares what colour that was?' he asked.

'I think that's horrible,' Polly said.

'Not at all. If she was so anxious to have the lamb going everywhere she did, the best thing she could do was to make sure it was inside her,' the wolf replied.

'Are all your songs about eating?' Polly asked.

'What else is there to make a song about?' the wolf asked, simply.

Polly considered the songs she knew. It did seem true that a great many of them were about eating. 'Little Jack Horner'. The Queen in 'Sing a Song of Sixpence'. 'Jack Sprat'. 'Goldilocks', with all those strawberries and cream. Even the pussycat who went to London to see the Queen had certainly eaten the little mouse she found there.

'The song about you is all about eating, too,' the wolf said.

'You mean, "Polly put the kettle on"?' Polly asked. She had always felt a little embarrassed by that song.

'Of course.'

'But it only says "tea". And I don't think it means a real sit-down tea you eat, with bread and butter and cake. I think it's only the sort of tea that comes out of a teapot,' Polly said.

'Nonsense. It's about quite a solid meal,' the wolf said. Polly repeated:

'Polly put the kettle on,
Polly put the kettle on,
Polly put the kettle on,
We'll all have tea.

If they'd been going to eat, it would say, butter the bread, or get out the cake tin.'

'What a miserable meal to ask your friends in to enjoy! Now, mine would really be quite something,' the wolf said.

'What does yours say?' Polly asked.

> *'Polly make the water hot,*
> *Polly make the water hot,*
> *Put it in a great big pot*
> *And then jump in . . .'*

'I wouldn't,' Polly said. The wolf took no notice. He went on:

> *'Clever wolf knows what to do,*
> *Leaves it for an hour or two,*
> *Gobbles up the Polly stew,*
> *It's all gone away.'*

'I wouldn't jump in. That would be stupid,' Polly said again.

'Exactly. That's what my mother said. I mean, she said you were stupid.'

'I haven't jumped into a pot of boiling water, have I?'

'Not yet,' the wolf said.

There was a short pause.

'She used to sing me a lullaby,' the wolf said, dreamily.

'Who did?'

'My mother. It was very soothing. Beautiful words, it had.

> *'Bye, baby bunting,*
> *Your father's gone a-hunting,*
> *He's gone to find a Polly in her*
> *Home to make your lovely dinner.'*

'He never did, though,' Polly said.

'He knew he could leave it to me,' the wolf said.

Polly picked up her recorder. She was finding this conversation either frightening or boring, she couldn't quite decide which.

'Are you going to play again?' the wolf asked, apprehensive.

Polly played the tune of 'Oranges and Lemons'. It was difficult and the notes did not always come out just as she meant them to.

'What's that tune?' the wolf asked, stretching his neck over the hedge.

'It's meant to be "Oranges and Lemons".'

'It sounds to me more like "Onions and Kidneys",' said the wolf.

'There isn't a tune called "Onions and Kidneys",' Polly said.

'Of course there is. It's a bit like what you were trying to play just then.'

'All right. Sing your song, then,' Polly said.

Not untunefully, the wolf sang:

> '*Onions and Kidneys*
> *Say the bells of St Sydney's.*
> *I'd like something sweeter,*
> *Says the bell of St Peter.*
> *Try our jam tarts,*
> *Say the bells of St Bart's.*
> *A well-roasted boy,*
> *Say the bells of St Foy.*

Poached girl on toast,
Is what we'd like most,
We'll have her for tea,
The bells all agree . . .'

'I don't agree,' Polly said quickly.

'That doesn't matter. If everyone else agrees, you get eaten. That's the law,' the wolf said. He bounded over the hedge and stood in the garden, immediately underneath Polly's window, his long red tongue lolling out of his mouth, his teeth wickedly agape.

'Lean further out of the window, Polly,' he said.

'I'm not allowed to. Mother says not to,' Polly said, primly.

'A pity. Never mind. Everyone agrees that you are there for me to eat. I shall wait until it is a little darker, and then I shall jump up and get you,' the wolf said, lying down, prepared to wait.

Polly thought quickly.

'I shouldn't advise you to wait too long, Wolf,' she said.

'What do you mean?'

'Only that it might be dangerous,' Polly said.

'Dangerous for you. Not for me,' the wolf said, in a self-satisfied voice.

'Wolf! Don't you know the song about "Boys and girls come out to play"?' Polly asked.

'Of course I know it. A stupid song. Something about a ha'penny loaf. Cubs' play,' the wolf snorted.

'I don't think your mother can have taught you the right words,' Polly said.

'My mother was a good wom . . . a good wolf. Don't say a word against her,' the wolf said.

'What words did she teach you for that song?' Polly asked.

The wolf closed his eyes and recited in a sing-song voice:

'*Girls and boys come out to play,*
The moon doth shine as bright as day.
Leave your supper and leave your sleep
And come with your playfellows in the street.
Come with a whoop and come with a call,
Come with a good will or come not at all.
Up the ladder and down the wall,
A ha' penny loaf will serve us all . . .

'I never cared for that,' the wolf said, shaking his shaggy head.

'And anyway, you've got it wrong,' Polly said.

'You mean there's more than a ha'penny loaf?' the wolf asked, interested.

'Something much better.

'*. . . Come with a whoop and come with a call,*
A well-cooked wolf will serve us all.
We'll roast his ribs and curry his tail,
And pickle his head in the salting pail,'

Polly finished.

There was a short silence. Then the wolf asked, 'What did you say was to be well cooked?'

'A wolf,' Polly said.

'Do boys and girls often eat wolf?'

'If it's well cooked. Especially at midnight feasts,' Polly said. She put the recorder to her mouth and thoughtfully played the first few bars of the tune.

The wolf jumped.

'Don't do that!' he said.

'Why not, Wolf? I'm just trying the tune over.'

'But suppose someone heard you? Suppose those boys and girls you mentioned . . . What would they think if they heard?'

'I suppose they might think there was something amusing going on in the street. After all, the moon is nearly as bright as day now. They might come with a whoop and a call,' Polly said.

'And if they did, they'd expect ... ? They might think that I was waiting for ... ? No! It's too horrible to imagine. Polly! May I ask a favour?' the wolf said, imploring.

'As long as you don't ask me to jump into a pot of boiling water,' Polly said.

'What a barbarous idea! Of course not. No. All I want is that you should refrain from trying out that dreadful tin trumpet ... I mean, would you be kind enough to do anything else but play those melodious tunes on your splendid instrument for the present? I ... I seem to have a headache. I require perfect silence. If you would just sit quietly there while I return home to take a couple of aspirins and go to bed with a hot-water bottle, I should be infinitely obliged,' the wolf said. He leapt over the hedge and started trotting fast down the road. As he went Polly heard him mutter to himself. 'Curry my tail! The idea! Pickle my head! I don't know what boys and girls are coming to.'

Polly shut the window. The evening was becoming chilly. She put the recorder away in its case and went down to supper. Baked beans and toast.

'Did you have a good practice?' her mother asked.

'Very good,' Polly said.

'Can you play "Begone Dull Care" for the school concert next week?'

'I expect so,' Polly said. And she thought to herself, 'Anyway, I can play "Begone Stupid Wolf" and make him go, too.'

5. Outside the Pet Shop

POLLY was standing outside the pet shop near her home and looking at the animals in cages in the windows. She liked the slant-eyed kittens, playing with each other, and the hamsters, sharing an apple. She was watching a tortoise, and wondering whether it was asleep or just feeling tired, when the person standing at her side suddenly spoke.

'Very boring,' the person said.

'What? What's boring?' Polly asked.

'All these creatures. Dull, boring, stupid,' the person said.

'The kittens aren't boring. Look at that stripy one trying to bite its own tail.'

'Kittens always do that. It's not amusing.'

'I think it's funny,' Polly said. The stripy kitten had managed to put a paw on the end of the tail it was chasing, and now tried to pounce on it and take it by surprise. As the kitten jumped, so did its tail, right out of reach. The kitten looked hurt and surprised.

'Silly little animals. Imagine not knowing where your own tail is. I would never want a kitten as a pet,' the person said.

'What would you want as a pet?' Polly asked. She was beginning to suspect that she knew who this person was, and she was quite interested to find out what sort of pet the wolf would choose for himself. She had a nasty suspicion that he might choose a juicy little girl, and that he wouldn't keep her as a pet for very long. He would probably turn her into his dinner.

'I certainly would not have a tortoise. They are boring, too. Asleep most of the time, and probably taste as uninteresting as they look,' the wolf said.

'The budgies aren't asleep. I wouldn't mind having a budgie,' Polly said.

'Hardly a mouthful ... I mean, their conversation is so limited. Imagine having to listen to nothing but tweet, tweet all day long.'

'I'd rather like a white mouse,' Polly said, pointing to a cage in which several mice were running over a wheel.

'Your ideas are so small. Why don't you go for something nearer your own size?'

'You mean, like a monkey?' Polly asked. She had once seen a monkey in the pet shop. It had sat in a too small cage, looking at all the passers-by with sad, hopeless eyes.

'Aha! It wasn't me that said you were like a monkey. It was you,' the wolf said, triumphant.

'I didn't! I just said that a monkey was larger than a white mouse.'

'I would not advise a monkey. Nasty, spiteful things. You never know when they'll turn and bite you. Not because they are hungry, in the ordinary way, but just to be horrible. Or pull your hair,' the wolf said.

'I've always thought I'd like a pony,' Polly said.

'How can you be so ... ordinary? Girls always want ponies.'

'I wouldn't mind a cat, even. Or a dog.'

'That's more ordinary still. Everyone has cats and dogs. Why don't you find a pet who is more interesting than a wretched cat or dog? Someone that no one else has thought of?'

'You mean, like a snake?'

'Of course not a snake. I wouldn't want a snake. Is that the best you can think of?' the wolf asked crossly.

'I'd rather like to have a baby crocodile. He could swim in my bath. Only I suppose when he grew up I wouldn't be able to keep him,' Polly said.

'You certainly wouldn't. If he was in the bath with you, there wouldn't be much left of you by the time you got out. I'm thinking of something quite different. Can't you guess what it is?'

'A dolphin? They are supposed to be very clever.'

'Not a dolphin. Why anybody should be interested in keeping a fish, I don't know. The animal I am thinking of is not a crocodile nor a budgie nor a dolphin. He is large. He has four legs. He has a tail and he is very, very clever. Much cleverer than any other animal you can think of,' the wolf said.

'Can he talk?'

'Of course he can talk. You ought to know that.'

'It's a parrot,' Polly said, forgetting about the four legs.

'It is not a parrot. Stupid, they are. All they can say is "Clever Polly". And that means nothing,' the wolf said quickly.

'A large animal. Very clever, with four legs. With big ears?' Polly asked.

'Big enough for him to hear everything worth listening to,' the wolf said, his own ears pricking up.

'A donkey,' Polly said.

'Grrr. Mind your manners. Donkeys are not clever. They are slow and obstinate. This creature is intelligent . . .'

'I know! It never forgets anything,' Polly cried.

'Right!' the wolf said.

'Has it got a long nose?'

'Long? It is not one of those snubby, useless little noses that you humans have. It is an elegant and very acute nose.'

'It's an elephant,' Polly said, sure that this time she had guessed right.

'It is not an elephant. Really, I can't remember when I met anyone with so little brain,' the wolf declared.

'Not a dolphin. Not a donkey. Not a snake. Not an elephant. Tell me something else about him,' Polly asked.

'This creature is remarkably sharp,' the wolf said.

'A hedgehog. Their prickles are very sharp.'

'Hedgehogs do not have fur.'

'You didn't say fur.'

'Didn't I? I must have forgotten. The animal I am thinking of has a thick coat of very elegant fur,' the wolf said.

'What colour?' Polly asked.

'Black. Black as ebony.'

'He's a mole. Moles have black velvet coats and long snouts.'

The wolf stamped with impatience. 'You can't really be so stupid. Moles are blind, or very nearly blind. They spend their time living underground. I . . . I mean, the animal I am thinking of, lives entirely above ground, in a very distinguished way . . .'

'Is he gentle?' Polly asked.

'As a lamb,' the wolf replied, showing his sharp yellow teeth in what he hoped was a pleasing smile.

'Does he know any tricks?'

'Tricks?' the wolf repeated, astonished.

'Does he catch lumps of sugar? Can he balance them on his nose? Does he beg for food?' Polly asked. She was enjoying this conversation.

'Certainly not. He has no need for such foolish games. Tricks, indeed! He is not a clown. And as for begging, of course not.

Why should an upright and self-respecting Wo . . . animal be forced to beg?'

'Well, what does he do? Why do you think he would make a good pet?' Polly asked.

'He is well brought up. Most people want their pets to be well brought up. He is large. Can take care of himself. He is faithful. He has been after . . . I mean, he has been following the same person for years. Never looks at anyone else.'

Polly thought about this.

'I see. This pet you are recommending is a large somebody, in a black fur coat. He has a long nose and large ears. He doesn't do any tricks, and he has been faithfully following the same someone for years. Is that right?'

'About right,' the wolf said.

'But if he has been after this someone for years and hasn't ever caught up with her, I don't see that he can be so very clever.'

'Ah! But if only she would take him into her house as a pet, she would soon discover just

how much cleverer . . . and more lovable, of
course, he is than she has ever realized,' the
wolf said.

'It's no good, Wolf. I don't want a large
black hairy pet, especially not one with long
ears and nose and a lot of very sharp teeth.
And my mother and father don't want me
to have a big pet who talks. They don't even
like my having a very small white mouse, or
a hamster. So, not today, thank you very
much,' Polly said, and she walked away

towards her home, leaving the wolf outside the pet shop, grinning in at the window and terrifying a harmless guinea-pig, who didn't at all care for that display of long yellow teeth, even if they were the other side of a plate-glass window.

6. The Trap

'WHAT do you think it's there for?' Polly said to her sister Jane. They were looking over the gate at an unusual object lying in the lane that ran along the side of their garden.

'Looks like a packing crate on its side,' Jane said.

'Why do you suppose its lid is tied back with that piece of string?'

'Don't know. Anyhow, it's very boring. And there's a horrible smell,' Jane said. She left Polly at the gate and went back into the house.

'I see you are admiring my tr . . . my latest piece of work,' the wolf said, appearing suddenly on the other side of the crate.

'I didn't realize it was yours, Wolf. What is it?' Polly asked.

'I can't tell you that, you stupid little girl. If I told you what it was for, it wouldn't take you by surprise, would it?' the wolf said crossly.

'Is it a present?' Polly asked. Surprises were sometimes presents, she knew.

'Certainly not. Why should I give you a present?' the wolf said.

Polly couldn't think of a good reason why he should. She asked, 'Why is the lid tied back with that bit of string?'

'Aha! That's what is so extremely clever. When someone goes into that tr . . . into that box to get the delicious lump of meat which I have placed at the further end, the string is loosened and the lid slams shut, and, hey presto! I have caught my prey.'

'And then what happens?' Polly asked.

'I go in and gobble her up. With the delicious piece of meat for afters,' the wolf said. He closed his eyes and licked his lips.

'Like a mousetrap?' Polly said.

'That's right. Like a mousetrap. But I am not trying to catch a mouse. I don't care much for mice. Too many whiskers and bones to be worth bothering with.'

'If it isn't for a mouse, who is it for?' Polly asked, though she had already guessed what sort of animal the wolf meant to catch in his trap.

'You ask too many questions. Why do you want to know?'

'I just wondered whether the animal you want to catch is interested in raw meat,' Polly said.

'Everyone is interested in raw meat,' the wolf said.

'I'm not.'

There was a short, appalled silence.

'Say that again,' the wolf said, presently.

'Say what?'

'You said . . . I thought that you said . . .
Perhaps my ears deceived me. I distinctly
thought I heard you say that you were not
interested in raw meat,' the wolf said.

'That's right. I don't like raw meat,' Polly
said.

'You mean that if you saw a delicious hunk
of raw meat at the further end of what looked
like a perfectly ordinary tr . . . wooden box,
you wouldn't go in and get it?' the wolf asked.
He could hardly believe what he heard.

'No. I wouldn't. Especially if it smelled like
what you've got in there,' Polly said.

There was a short silence.

'Ah well! One lives and learns. I must be
getting along, now. Nice to have seen you,
Polly. No doubt we shall be meeting again,'
the wolf said sadly, as he turned away along
the lane, dragging the unsuccessful trap
behind him.

'He'll be back,' Polly thought. She had had
experience with the wolf before. She knew

how difficult it was for him to give up an idea
that had once seemed a good one.

'Road's up again,' Polly's father said, coming
in, cross, after a long drive home, to find a
large hole in the road just outside his own
garage.

'What is it this time? Gas? Electricity?
Drains?' Polly's mother asked, ladling out hot
soup into bowls for the family.

'Didn't ask. Wasn't anyone there. No lights,
no signs. Disgrace,' Polly's father said.

'I'll have a look tomorrow. Take care. Soup's
hot,' Polly's mother said, a little too late.
Polly's father had already burned his tongue.

The next morning, after breakfast, Polly
looked out from her garden and saw the hole in
the road. As her father had said, there were no
protective barriers and no lamps. There was
only one workman, a large person in blue
dungarees, hacking away at the road surface
with an old-fashioned pickaxe.

'Why are you digging that hole?' Polly called from the gate.

The person stopped his digging and looked towards her. He shook his head without speaking and lifted the pickaxe for another stroke.

'Is it for the electricity? Or the gas? Or the water?' Polly asked.

'Never you mind what it's for. Ask no questions and you won't hear any lies,' the person said, a little out of breath with the effort he had been making.

Polly considered this. Some people, she thought, told lies without being asked questions.

'Is it going to be a much larger hole?' she asked presently, as the workman drove smaller holes in the road surrounding the first one.

'It will be enormous,' the workman said. He jumped on a crumbling edge and said, 'Ow!' as he disappeared. The edge had given way under his feet. A moment later the top of his head appeared on a level with the road surface.

'Did you see that?' he asked, scrambling up out of the hole.

'I wish you'd tell me what the hole is for,' Polly said.

'Can't tell you that,' the workman said, raising his pickaxe for another stroke.

'Is it a secret?' Polly asked. She loved secrets.

'It's a secret,' the workman agreed. He raised his pickaxe again and brought it down with an immense thump into the hole in the road.

There was a hiss, a rush, a roar. Polly took several steps back into her garden, as a column of water, perhaps ten feet high, shot up from the water-mains pipe which the pickaxe had hit. The workman stood under a shower-bath of falling water, while the road at his feet rapidly turned to a flowing river of mud.

'Waugh! Whoosh! Atishoo!' the person said, trying to struggle free of the cascade of water. 'Why don't you *do* something? Hoosh!' he said, angrily, to the dry and interested Polly on the further side of the garden hedge.

'Engineers! Police! Fire Brigade!' the person spluttered. He reached for his pickaxe and aimed a furious blow at the point where the water was spurting. There was a deafening explosion. Blue flames crackled across the waterfall. The person had managed to hit not only the water mains, but also the electric cable.

An angry woman appeared on the doorstep of a neighbouring house.

'My electric has gone out! You've cut off my electric!' she said, pointing at the wet and bedraggled workman.

'I never touched your electric,' the workman said.

'It's gone off! And there was my nice chicken, only half cooked,' the woman said.

'Did you say a half-cooked chicken?' the person said, eagerly. He was drenched, he was singed, but he was also hungry. Water was still gushing up under his feet, but he seemed hardly to notice this.

'I'll telephone 999,' Polly said. But when she reached the telephone in her house, she found that it was dead. The person digging a hole in the road had cut through the telephone wires as well as everything else. After this the road was barricaded off for several days while men from the Metropolitan Water Board, from the London Electricity Board and from the Post Office came and mended all the different bits and put the surface of the road back again.

'That wasn't very clever, Wolf,' Polly said, looking out of a first-floor window and seeing the wolf sadly gazing at the large knobbly patch in the road where, not so long ago, he had dug his ill-fated hole.

'How could I know there were all those pipes and wires and things just there?' he grumbled, kicking a loose stone crossly into the gutter.

'Haven't you ever seen men digging up the road? Or sometimes it's the pavement. There are always lots of pipes and wires, all muddled up together.'

'No one told me,' the wolf said sulkily.

'Anyway, why were you digging that hole? Were you trying to get down to Australia?' Polly asked.

'My dear Polly! Don't you know that Australia is on the other side of the world? Twenty thousand miles away, or something like that?'

'I just thought perhaps you thought you could get there by digging straight through,' Polly said.

'Straight through all those tangled-up wires and things? No, thank you. Anyhow, if Australia is twenty thousand miles away, how could it be at the bottom of a hole that I'm digging here?'

'Because the world is round. Australia is directly underneath us,' Polly said.

The wolf sighed loudly.

'I don't know whether you are really as stupid as you pretend, or if you make these things up to annoy me. Of course the world isn't round. Anyone can see it's flat. If it was round,' the wolf went on, thinking hard, 'some of the people would be falling off all the time. They'd be upside down. Stop talking nonsense. If you can,' he added grimly.

'Well, what were you digging that hole for?' Polly asked.

'That's a secret.'

'Is it a secret now, when it isn't there any longer?' Polly asked.

'It certainly is. It was part of a very clever plan, which I shall carry out successfuly at another time and in another place,' the wolf said.

'If you want to dig a big hole, why don't you try something easier than the road? Why don't you dig in the earth? On the Heath, for instance?' Polly asked.

The wolf considered this suggestion. Then he asked, 'Do you often go for walks on the Heath?'

'Nearly every day.'

'Goodbye, Polly. I have just remembered some urgent business. I hope we shall meet again soon,' the wolf said, and Polly saw him hurry away down the road in the direction of the Heath. She had a very good idea of what his urgent business was going to be.

Sure enough, a few days later, when she was coming home with her sisters from walking across the Heath, she heard loud puffing sounds, and saw someone working hard on a small patch of grass surrounded by low bushes.

'Hi!' the someone called as the three girls came near.

'What do you want?' Polly called back, prudently keeping the bushes between herself and the working person.

'Come here and see what I'm doing. No. That isn't what I mean. Come here and see what I'm not doing. No. That's not right, either. Come here and don't see what I'm doing,' the wolf said, leaning on his spade.

'You mean come right up to you and don't look?'

'That's right,' the wolf said, pleased.

'You want me to walk towards you but to look somewhere else?' Polly said.

'You could shut your eyes. In fact, that would be the best way to do it,' the wolf said.

'I don't think I'm clever enough to walk straight through between the bushes with my eyes shut,' Polly said.

'How terrible it must be for you to be so very, very stupid,' the wolf said, showing his teeth in a large smile.

'Could you do it?' Polly asked.

'Of course.'

'Perhaps if you showed me how, I would be able to copy you,' Polly suggested.

'Dead easy,' the wolf said.

'Show me, then,' Polly said.

The wolf went to the far side of the patch of grass inside the ring of bushes. He shut his eyes.

'Like this,' he said.

'And then what happens?' Polly asked.

'You just step boldly forward and walk across this fine grassy space. Like so,' the wolf said, and he stepped forward.

'I think it's time we went back to tea,' Polly said to her sisters. As they turned towards home, they heard behind them a sudden loud cry.

'What's that?' Lucy asked, stopping short.

'Perhaps someone has fallen down,' said Jane.

'Into a large hole,' Polly said.

'Why should anyone dig a very large hole and then fall into it?' Lucy asked.

'Because,' Polly answered, 'he is not a very clever wolf.'

7. The Wolf Goes Wooing (1)

'AT LAST I see where I've been mistaken,' the wolf said. He was reading one of his favourite books, a collection of stories about clever animals, princes and princesses, wicked witches and terrible dragons. His old mother had given it to him when he was nothing more than a young cub and had told him that everything he needed to know would be found in this excellent book.

'The mistake I've made has been to try to catch Polly by tricks. I've tried to take her by surprise. To pounce. Of course she has always run away. Now I understand the right way of going about it, I shall try a quite different method,' the wolf said to himself.

A few days later, Polly was sitting on the swing in the front garden when she saw the wolf walking carefully down the road. On his head he wore a small crown of gold-coloured paper. In one hand he carried a short stick. When he reached the garden gate he stopped and leaned over it.

'Good afternoon, Polly,' he said.

'Good afternoon, Wolf,' Polly replied.

'I hope you are well,' the wolf said.

'I'm very well, thank you, Wolf.'

'I wonder . . .' the wolf said, looking round. His eye fell on a flower-bed of tulips which had been carefully planted there several months before, by Polly's mother.

'I wonder if you would be kind enough to get me a glass of water? I've come a long way in the heat and dust,' he said.

Polly was a kind girl. When the wolf put out a long red tongue, turned his eyes upwards and panted thirstily, she didn't like to refuse. She went into the house and came out in two or three minutes' time, carrying a tumbler of cold water. To her surprise, when she offered it to the wolf, he didn't immediately take it. Instead he handed her a large bunch of bright yellow tulips.

'For the fairest in the land,' he said, bowing. His paper crown fell off. He quickly picked it up and put it back, tipped crazily over one ear.

Polly looked round the garden.

'Wolf! They're our tulips. You've picked them all. They're Mother's best flowers. She'll be furious,' she said.

'Nothing is too good for a beautiful princess like you,' the wolf said, not seeming to care about Polly's mother.

'And I'm not a princess,' Polly said.

'To me you will always be a princess. And I'm a prince. Can't you see my crown? And my sceptre?' the wolf asked. He pointed to the lop-sided paper crown and flourished the small stick in his left paw.

'I don't understand . . .' Polly began.

'You can't help being stupid,' the wolf agreed. Then, remembering his new idea, he added quickly, 'Not stupid. Just a little slow to understand the new situation, perhaps.'

'What am I supposed to do with these?' Polly asked, looking at the bunch of tulips in dismay.

'Put them in water, of course,' the wolf said, taking the flowers from her and plunging them into the tumbler of water which Polly had brought from the house.

'I thought you were so hot and thirsty,' Polly said.

'That was a cunning trick so that you would go into the house and I could pick these beautiful flowers for you,' the wolf said, very much pleased with himself.

'Why do you want to give me flowers?'

'Aha!' the wolf said.

'Aha what?' Polly asked.

'Aha! I have a new plan. I see now, Polly, that I have been wrong in trying to catch you unawares. I shouldn't have tried to take you by surprise. The right thing to do with beautiful young girls is not to pounce, but to approach them gently. To woo them. That is why I have come here today to give you flowers. And the usual three gifts, of course,' the wolf said.

'The usual three gifts? What are they?' Polly asked.

'According to my book, always things that are very difficult to find. For instance, the smallest dog in the world. Or the most beautiful princess. But of course, I don't have to go looking for her, because that's you,' the wolf said in a hurry.

'What else?' Polly asked, interested.

'You might ask me to build a superb palace outside your gates in a single night.'

'Would you be able to do that?'

'I should have a very good try,' the wolf said modestly.

'Are there any other gifts to choose from?'

'You might want a golden bird. Or the water of life. Or a dress made of moonshine,' the wolf said.

'You mean you could find any of those things?'

'Of course. A prince can always accomplish the task that has been set for him,' the wolf replied.

'Like killing a dragon?' Polly asked.

The wolf hesitated. Then he said, 'Are there any dragons around here nowadays? As far as you know?'

'I don't think there are many. But it's one of the things brave princes often have to do before they get the princess.'

'Does your father have any special dragon in mind? A reasonably mild dragon, who wouldn't object to putting up some sort of fight, just for the look of it? And who would then pretend to be defeated and to die? Just for a short time, you understand. Something like that?' the wolf asked.

'No, I don't think my father knows any dragons,' Polly said.

'Any of the neighbours been complaining about having dragons in the garden lately? Or in the house?' the wolf inquired.

'Not that I've heard,' Polly said.

'Then let's forget about dragons, shall we? If nobody round here is being bothered by dragons at present, there doesn't seem much point in going out and looking for them. Let sleeping dragons lie, is what my old aunt always said. Or, indeed, die. Let sleeping dragons die. Peacefully, in their lairs. We don't want to cause any disturbances, do we?'

Polly remembered some of the earlier attempts the wolf had made to catch her. She didn't feel sure that he had always tried to avoid disturbing people. There had been the time when he had meant to blow up her house, which wasn't exactly a peaceful occupation.

'Well? Which is it to be? The palace? The golden bird? The smallest dog in the world? Which do you want first?' the wolf asked.

'I think I'd like the smallest dog, please,' Polly said. She had not forgotten that she would never be allowed to keep a large pet. A very small dog might perhaps be hidden in her toy cupboard. Or, if he was small enough, even in the box where she kept her special treasures.

'I shall be back tomorrow,' the wolf said. And went.

It was late in the afternoon of the next day that the wolf arrived at Polly's garden gate. He was again wearing the paper crown, but this time he had left the stick behind and instead, in his paw, he was carrying a brown paper bag.

He leaned over the gate.

'Polly!'

'Yes, Wolf?'

'I have brought you what I promised. The smallest dog in the world.'

He handed Polly the brown paper bag. She looked eagerly inside.

'There isn't any tiny dog. Just a lot of nuts,' she said.

'Of course. Who ever heard of keeping tiny dogs loose in paper bags? They'd get terribly tangled up in each other's legs. Don't you know that the smallest dog in the world always comes out of a nut?' the wolf said.

'I don't know that I'll be allowed to keep so many dogs,' Polly said, looking into the bag again. There were at least forty hazelnuts there.

'I daresay there won't be a dog inside every single nut. You know what they say. Don't count your nuts until they are cracked,' the wolf said.

'Do you know which nuts have dogs and which haven't?' Polly asked.

'Not exactly. They look rather alike. We'd better open a few . . .'

'I'll go and fetch the nut-crackers,' Polly said, starting for the house.

'Oh no, you don't. I know what you mean to do. You'll go into the house and never come out again. I can crack nuts with my teeth,' the wolf said.

'I've always been told not to try,' Polly said.

'You have such small teeth. Feeble. Now, choose your nut, and I'll crack it open for you,' the wolf said.

Polly took a nut from the bag and handed it to the wolf. The wolf cracked it between his teeth and held out the two halves of the shell to Polly. But inside was no tiny dog, only an ordinary nut kernel.

'You picked the wrong one,' the wolf accused Polly.

'You said they all looked alike,' Polly reminded him.

'Let's try another,' the wolf said.

The second nut also had nothing but a kernel inside. The wolf quickly ate it. He pointed to the paper bag, and Polly brought out a third. But this one contained nothing at all.

'Perhaps they're the wrong sort of nut,' Polly suggested.

'Nonsense. The book says quite clearly that the smallest dog in the world came out of a hazelnut. The trouble is that you haven't found the right one. Get on with it. He must be in there, somewhere,' the wolf said.

As fast as he could crack them, the wolf opened nut after nut. But each one proved disappointingly to be nothing but a perfectly ordinary hazelnut. Most of them had kernels, which the wolf quickly swallowed. He did not offer Polly any. Faster and faster the shells fell around him, and he had hardly eaten one kernel before he was cracking the next nut. The supply in the bag dwindled until there was only one nut left. Polly was just taking it out of the bag, when suddenly the wolf spluttered and choked.

'Hauch! Hawk! Haroosh! Ahaugh! A-haugh! A-choo! Hauch! Hack! Harrock!' the wolf exclaimed.

'Did it go down the wrong way?' Polly asked.

The wolf coughed and nodded his head. He still couldn't speak.

Polly waited till he had recovered. Then she said, 'Wolf! There's only one nut left.'

'Splendid. Then this is THE nut. Prepare to meet the smallest dog in the world.'

The wolf cracked the last nut with great care. He spat out the shell and held out his paw with the contents of the nut on it for Polly to see.

'It's not a tiny dog,' Polly said.

'Are you quite sure?' the wolf asked.

'Quite. It's just an ordinary nut kernel. Like in all the other nuts,' Polly said.

'There must be another nut left,' the wolf said.

Polly looked in the paper bag.

'No. That was the very last one.'

The wolf scratched his head.

'Extraordinary! Out of all those nuts, not one containing the smallest dog in the world! Not one of them, in fact, containing a dog of any sort or size.'

He thought about this.

'I suggest that we forget about the dog. Or, better still, we do a deal. After all, I did bring you a great many nuts. Suppose we say that twenty nuts count the same as one very small dog? That would be generous. Considering the size of the dog.'

'No. It has to be the smallest dog in the world, or it doesn't count at all,' Polly said.

'Of course! I was forgetting. One of those nuts did contain the smallest dog in the world,' the wolf cried.

'I didn't see it,' Polly said.

'No. Most unfortunately, you didn't. Why? Because, entirely by mistake, I swallowed him. He was in that last nut but one. The nut that went down the wrong way. You remember?'

'I remember. But . . .' Polly said.

'That was the smallest dog in the world.'

'How do I know that?' Polly asked.

'If it wasn't, why was that the only nut that made me choke? All the others went down the way they should have gone. But the dog inside that nut didn't just follow down the long red lane like an ordinary kernel. He chose a different path. I remember now the feeling on my tongue. As if a very small animal was trotting across it. In the wrong direction,' the wolf said.

'I don't believe it,' Polly said.

'I also heard him bark. Before he'd got right down. You must have heard him too.'

'I didn't . . .'

'But you must agree that that nut was quite different from all the others,' the wolf urged.

'Because you were in too much of a hurry.'

'He was in too much of a hurry. That's the trouble about these very small dogs. They don't wait to find out what would be best for them.'

'Anyway, you haven't given me any sort of dog,' Polly said.

'I brought him here,' the wolf protested.

'And then you ate him.'

'It was a mistake. I didn't mean to,' the wolf cried. But it was no good. Polly had gone into the house and shut the door.

'I shall be back. Tomorrow I shall be here with the second gift,' the wolf promised. 'I'll probably be building you a palace tomorrow,' he said to the firmly shut door.

But Polly did not come out again, and the wolf went sadly home.

8. The Wolf Goes Wooing (2)

'POLLY! I have come with the second gift,' the wolf said, from his usual place outside the garden gate.

'That's very kind of you, Wolf,' Polly said.

'Come a little nearer and I will lay it at your feet.'

'I'll come this near. That's enough,' Polly said, standing a little distance from the gate. The day before, when she had gone right up to the gate to hand the wolf a glass of water, and again to look into a paper bag, hoping to see the smallest dog in the world, she had forgotten how little he was to be trusted.

'It's sad that you should be so young and so suspicious,' the wolf said.

'It would be sadder still if I weren't suspicious and never lived to be not so young,' Polly said.

'Ah well. Let's talk about something else. I have brought you the second of the three gifts with which I am going to win you.'

'What is it?' Polly asked.

The wolf held up a string bag.

'It was quite extraordinary. I thought that this task might be the most difficult. I wondered if it might not prove impossible. But I'm delighted to be able to tell you that one can buy them anywhere. They are not even very expensive.'

'What are they?' Polly asked. She was impatient to know what the second gift could be.

The wolf put a paw into the bag and took out a large yellow apple.

'Golden apples.' He rolled one under the gate towards Polly. She picked it up.

'I don't think this apple is made of gold, Wolf,' she said.

'Excuse me. I have the shopkeeper's word for it. "What are those apples?" I asked, and he said, "They are Golden."'

Polly took a large bite out of the apple. 'I wouldn't be able to do that if they were really made of solid gold,' she said.

'There must be some mistake. Perhaps the next one . . .' the wolf said, rummaging in the bag. He took out a second apple. It looked exactly like the first.

'That one isn't gold either. Bite it and see,' Polly said.

'Oh no! You don't catch me that way! You want me to be stupid enough to try to bite an apple made of real gold, so that I blunt my teeth. Then I shouldn't ever be able to eat you up like a piece of crisp bacon. Oh, no!'

'Just as you like. Don't eat it then. But it's a waste, because even if these apples aren't really golden, they are delicious.'

'That's what the shopkeeper said. He said they were golden *and* delicious,' the wolf said. He smelled the apple in his paw and cautiously scraped it against his teeth. A moment later the second apple had disappeared.

'The third apple must be the golden one. The man very kindly gave me two delicious apples, and one, this last one, is golden. You couldn't expect more than that for thirty pence,' the wolf said as soon as his mouth was empty enough to speak.

'That apple isn't golden either,' Polly said, looking at it as the wolf drew it from the string bag.

'But the shopkeeper assured me . . .' the wolf began. Polly interrupted him.

'Wolf! This sort of apple is called Golden Delicious. That's its name. Like I'm called Polly. Like other apples are called Coxes, or

Granny Smiths. This yellow sort of apple is called Golden Delicious. It doesn't mean that they are really made of gold,' Polly said.

'Why didn't he explain properly? I told him distinctly that I wanted golden apples, and he sells me these stupid things,' the wolf said, angry. He threw the third apple over the gate. It rolled across the grass to the sandpit, where small fat Lucy was sitting, burying a doll she didn't care for. Without looking up, Lucy picked up the apple and began to eat it.

'Now that horrible child is eating my last apple. I am leaving you. Grieved. Hurt. Disappointed. But I shall be back soon with the third and last gift,' the wolf said, turning away from the gate. He took off the gilt paper crown. He obviously thought it was no longer necessary to pretend to be a prince come a-wooing on this occasion. He threw the string bag over his shoulder and trotted away down the road.

Polly wondered what the third and last gift would be. In the stories she had read there were certainly three gifts, but she couldn't guess which the wolf would choose to bring. A magic ring would be useful. So would a cloak that made the wearer invisible. Best of all would be Fortunatus's purse, which always had a gold coin in it, however much you spent from it. 'But I hope he doesn't bring me a beautiful princess. I wouldn't know what to do with her,' Polly thought.

It was nearly a week later, on a fine and sunny afternoon, when Polly, sitting on the grass in the front garden, and colouring a large picture of a hungry dragon and a beautiful princess, heard a curious sound from the other side of the hedge.

She went up and peered through the leaves and twigs.

Outside in the road the wolf was standing. He seemed to be speaking to someone, but who the someone was, Polly couldn't see.

'Why not?' the wolf asked.

There was no answer.

'Just this one more, and I'll never ask for another,' the wolf said.

No reply.

'You owe it to me. I bought you. I paid good money for you. You belong to me. It's your duty to do what I tell you,' the wolf scolded.

Polly edged closer to the privet hedge. The wolf seemed to be speaking to someone below him, right down on the road level. Perhaps, Polly thought, he had at last discovered the smallest dog in the world.

But she didn't see a dog of any size. Instead she saw, lying on the road, a little piece of material. It was about the size of a small sheet of newspaper. It was torn at the edges and not very clean. But as Polly looked carefully, she saw that it was a ragged fragment of a very old, very worn Persian carpet. She could just make out a pattern of something like little trees and, round one frayed corner, a border of zigzag lines.

'I could easily bite you and tear you up into shreds,' the wolf said angrily to the carpet.

The carpet shrugged. If you have never seen a carpet shrug, I can tell you that it is a very expressive gesture.

'It was only a very short journey this morning. You can't be that tired,' the wolf pleaded.

The carpet gave an irritated shake, as much as to say, 'Stop bothering me.'

Polly went to the garden gate and leaned over so that she could see both the wolf and the carpet, and the wolf, if not the carpet, could see her.

'What's the trouble, Wolf?' she asked.

The wolf picked up the fragment of carpet, came to the further side of the gate, and slapped the carpet down on the white, dusty road in front of it.

'It's extremely annoying. I managed to find the third and last gift I promised you. This flying carpet. Or rather, this part of the original flying carpet.'

'It's not very large,' Polly said, looking at the small square of carpet.

'That's the trouble. It claims that because it is only a small piece of the whole carpet, it can no longer fly as often or as quickly as it used to,' the wolf said.

'But it does fly?' Polly asked.

'Only when it feels like it.'

The carpet wrinkled itself.

'Don't laugh at me!' the wolf cried, stamping an angry paw.

The carpet's wrinkles became deeper and it quivered with silent laughter.

'Maddening! You . . . you ordinary *rug*!' the wolf shouted. Instantly the carpet flew off the ground and slapped the wolf smartly on the nose, covering him at the same time with a good deal of white dust and small pebbles which it had managed to pick up from the road.

The wolf coughed and then sneezed. The carpet, back on the ground, gave a wriggle. It was clearly saying, 'Mind your manners, you!'

The wolf tried again.

'I beg your pardon. Of course I meant to say, this beautiful, elegant, clever carpet can fly anywhere and at any time, but being old . . . I mean to say, being a carpet of great experience and wisdom, sometimes needs to rest quietly. In order to preserve its magic power. You understand?'

The carpet spread itself out on the road and preened itself.

'Has it flown anywhere with you?' Polly asked.

'Of course. I couldn't bring you a flying carpet without first trying it out. I suggested that it should lift me from the ground. It was a mistake, though, to try the experiment in my kitchen, where the ceiling is rather low,' the wolf said, rubbing the top of his head.

The carpet wrinkled again. It was clearly amused at the memory. The wolf wisely pretended not to have seen.

'Since then, things haven't been too easy. This miser . . . this beautiful carpet does not feel able to take me to any place and at any time, as it could have done in the olden days, when it was all there. I mean, when more than this precious fragment was at hand. As you probably remember from reading your "Arabian Nights", the whole carpet could transport any number of people as far as they chose to ask. And at any time. This . . . this treasured remnant is apparently too old and too tired to answer to the command in the same way. It needs to rest very often. In fact, it seems to be resting, doing nothing, most of the time,' the wolf said, showing his teeth in a threatening manner.

The carpet hunched itself, ready to spring for the wolf's nose.

'Of course I understand this. Real magic is very tiring. We don't want to strain it,' the wolf said hastily.

The carpet flattened itself out again.

'But there it is, Polly. A truly magic flying carpet. You can't say I haven't done what I promised. I said I would bring you three gifts, and I have. I have won you, Polly. By all the rules in the book, you are now mine,' the wolf said. He leaned over the garden gate and put a large black paw on Polly's shoulder.

'Wait a moment, Wolf. Those three gifts. I never even saw the smallest dog in the world,' Polly said.

'He was extremely small. You weren't wearing your spectacles, so you missed him,' the wolf said.

'I don't need spectacles. I didn't see him because he wasn't there.'

'But you heard him. He barked loudly when I swallowed him. Quite by accident. He came out of his nut too quickly. It was entirely his own fault.'

'I heard you spluttering,' Polly said.

'That wasn't me. That was the noise he made as he went down,' the wolf said.

'And the apples weren't real gold,' Polly said.

'The best gold is always soft. I think you didn't keep them long enough. You and your horrible sister were so anxious to eat them up directly you saw them, you didn't give them a chance to harden up. Greed is very unattractive,' the wolf said virtuously.

'Anyway, I don't believe that carpet can really fly,' Polly said.

'You saw it come up and hit me on the nose just now.'

'That could have been a trick.'

Two corners of the square of carpet lifted a little, looking like two ears pricked up on a dog's head.

'Come out here and stand on it. Say, "I wish you to take me to the wolf's kitchen" and you'll see,' the wolf said.

'That's hardly any way. I could walk there, easily . . .'

'Do!' the wolf said eagerly, but Polly took no notice.

'If it's really a magic flying carpet it ought to be able to take me to the other side of the world,' she said.

'It can.'

'How do I know it can?' Polly asked. The carpet wriggled. It knew it was being talked about.

'Try it. Ask it nicely, and I am sure it will oblige. So long as it isn't still too tired.'

'If I do, and it does take me to the other side of the world, I think I'll stay there for a bit and look around,' Polly said.

'That wouldn't do at all. I need you here,' the wolf said.

'Then why don't you ask it to take you somewhere? Then I'd see that it really is a magic carpet,' Polly suggested.

The wolf moved towards the carpet. He sat carefully on its middle, legs crossed. It was a tight fit. He had to hold his tail very close, in order to tuck himself neatly on to the very small piece of carpet, with no bits hanging over the edges.

'Take me to my kitchen,' he said.

The carpet did not stir.

'Oh, all right! *Please*,' the wolf said.

The carpet wriggled.

'Don't do that. You're tickling me underneath,' the wolf said.

Polly waited.

'I don't believe it can fly at all,' she said.

'Don't say that. You might hurt its feelings and goodness knows what it might do. You have to be polite. Like this. Please, beautiful, clever, kind carpet, take me to . . . to Brighton,' the wolf said.

The carpet shuddered.

'I don't think it likes the idea of going to Brighton. Perhaps it doesn't like all those pebbles on the beach. Or it's frightened of getting wet in the sea. Why don't you suggest that it takes you somewhere it would like to go to? Like its own home?' Polly suggested.

The wolf looked hard at her.

'Sometimes, Polly, I think you have the glimmerings of intelligence. That is not a bad suggestion,' he said. He patted the carpet gently. 'Elegant, superb, gifted, wonderful carpet, grant me this one wish and I'll never ask you for anything again. Fly with me to your native land, to Persia, to your home.'

There was a rush of air, a column of white dust, a short yelp of surprise, and then silence. The road beyond Polly's garden gate was empty. Only a small clean square on the dusty ground remained to show where the flying carpet had once lain.

'I wonder,' thought clever Polly, 'how the wolf is going to get home from Persia? Because I'm quite sure the carpet won't ever agree to bring him back.'

Extra!

Extra!

READ ALL ABOUT IT!

CATHERINE STORR

TALES OF
POLLY
THE HUNGRY

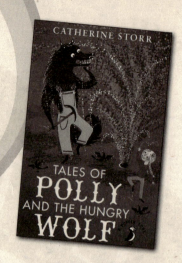

1913   *Born Catherine Cole on 21 July in Kensington,
        London*

1924–31 *Catherine is a pupil at St Paul's Girls' School
        in London where she is lucky enough to be
        taught by Gustav Holst, the music teacher at
        the school, learning to play the piano and the
        organ, eventually becoming the organist for the
        daily morning service at the school*

1931   *Catherine is accepted at Newnham College,
        Cambridge, where she studies English literature*

1937   *Catherine writes her first children's story,
        Ingeborg and Ruthy. Ruthy was the name of her
        much-loved doll as a child*

1940   *Ingeborg and Ruthy is published by George
        G. Harrap & Co. Catherine returns to*

Cambridge to study medicine. At Cambridge she meets and falls in love with Anthony Storr, a fellow medical student

1942   *Catherine and Anthony marry*

1944   *Catherine and Anthony qualify as doctors. Both also start training in psychiatry. Catherine gives birth to the first of three daughters*

1950–63 *Catherine works part-time as a senior medical officer in the Department of Psychological Medicine at the Middlesex Hospital and also writes stories for children. As her daughters grow older, she writes books for older children*

1952   *Her first two books are published:* Stories for Jane *and* Clever Polly, and other stories

1955   Clever Polly and the Stupid Wolf *is published and becomes hugely popular*

1957   *A sequel,* Polly and the Wolf Again, *is published*

1958   Marianne Dreams, *a novel for older children, is published. It has remained in print ever since and has been published in many foreign languages*

1960   Marianne and Mark *(the sequel to* Marianne Dreams*) is published*

1961   *Catherine helps to set up the Charlotte M. Yonge Society, devoted to studying the Victorian*

novelist *who was a bestselling author of her time*

1966   *Takes on a new job as an editor at Penguin Books and continues writing*

1971   Thursday, *a novel for young adults, is published*

2001   *Catherine dies aged eighty-seven on 8 January in London; her last book is published in the autumn*

INTERESTING FACTS

Catherine Storr wrote her first children's books for her three daughters – Sophia, Polly and Emma.

She also wrote *Marianne Dreams*, a book for 9–12 year olds.

ABOUT THE ILLUSTRATOR

JILL BENNETT

Jill Bennett *was born in Johannesburg, South Africa, in 1934. She began drawing from an early age and always wanted to be a children's book illustrator. She also loved the theatre and studied at Wimbledon School of Art, specializing in Theatre Design, and the Slade School of Fine Art. Jill went on to illustrate many wonderful children's stories by authors such as Roald Dahl and Dick King-Smith.*

Jill is also the creator of exquisitely detailed miniature dolls that have been displayed in museums all over the world.

INTERESTING FACTS

Jill was the first illustrator of Roald Dahl's *Fantastic Mr Fox* and later *Danny the Champion of the World*.

WHERE DID THE STORY COME FROM?

Catherine's daughter – the real Polly – says:

'My sisters and I were very lucky that our mother, Catherine Storr, had a wonderful imagination and the desire to be a writer. Our childhood was full of stories told or read to us. When I was five or six my family visited Whipsnade Zoo which had a wood where wild wolves lived. I remember looking through the chain link fence into the dark wood and seeing wolves slinking through the trees like ominous shadows. I was very frightened by the wolves, and my fears continued after we returned home. So my mother wrote a short story for me called "Clever Polly" in which Polly avoids a wolf's efforts to eat her by outwitting him. This story was the first of many more about Clever Polly and the Stupid Wolf.'

WORDS GLORIOUS WORDS!

Lots of words have several different meanings – here are a few you'll find in this Puffin Book. Use a **dictionary** or look them up online to find other definitions.

agape *a mouth wide open in surprise*

apprehensive *afraid that something bad will happen*

barbarous *extremely harsh and brutal*

refrain *to not do something you were going to do*

bedraggled *in a messy state*

declaimed *spoken with strong feeling and in a loud voice*

caterwauling *screeching*

GUESS
WHO?

A *On his head he wore a small crown of gold-coloured paper. In one hand he carried a short stick.*

B *She hadn't been learning very long, and she could only play easy tunes.*

C *'Told you, we don't keep them. They're out of date.'*

D *'Here! Move off, can't you? No one asked you to join the party.'*

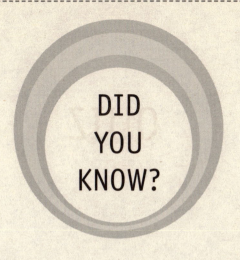

DID YOU KNOW?

The **Grey** wolf is the name of the most common Wolf species. However, **Arctic** grey wolves have fur that's as **white** as snow so that they blend in with the Arctic environment, while wolves that live in warmer places range in colour from **grey-white, brown,** and different shades of **black.**

Wolves have very powerful senses of smell, sight and hearing. In fact a wolf's sense of smell is more than 100 **times greater** than a human's.

Wolves have a lot of teeth – 42 **altogether.** Wolves are highly **intelligent!**

QUIZ

1 In 'The Spell' what 'magic' product does the wolf buy in the food store?

a) Frozen meat

b) Bread

c) Biscuits

d) Meat tenderizer

2 How many stout ladies are there in 'The Enchanted Polly?

a) Two

b) Three

c) Four

d) Five

3 *In 'Songs My Mother Taught Me', what does Polly have for supper after practising her recorder?*

a) *Tomato soup*

b) *Baked beans on toast*

c) *Fish fingers*

d) *Cheese and crackers*

4 *What animal does the wolf recommend as a good pet in 'Outside the Pet Shop'?*

a) *A budgie*

b) *A crocodile*

c) *A dolphin*

d) *A wolf*

5 *What type of flowers does the wolf present to Polly as a gift in 'The Wolf Goes Woo-ing?*

a) *Pansies*

b) *Roses*

c) *Tulips*

d) *Daffodils*

MAKE AND DO

Grow your own pot of tulips!

The best time of year to plant tulip bulbs is in late autumn, and by spring you will have a beautiful display of tulips!

YOU WILL NEED:

* A packet of bulbs
* Pots
* Compost
* Water
* Small stones

1   *Put a few small stones in the bottom of the pot for drainage.*

2   *Cover the stones with a layer of compost, about a third deep, depending on the size of the pot.*

3   *Plant two or three tulip bulbs (or more if it's a large pot) with the pointed end up, the roots down.*

4   *Cover to the top with more compost.*

5   *Label your pots and leave outside until the spring when they will start to shoot up.*

IN THIS YEAR

The first ever **Rubik's Cube** goes on sale.

Margaret Thatcher is Britain's **first female** Prime Minister.

Star Wars Episode V: The Empire Strikes Back is released in cinemas.

PUFFIN
WRITING
TIP

From A to Z write a word that goes with every letter in the alphabet and then pick your favourite to write about!

If you have enjoyed *Tales of Clever Polly and the Hungry Wolf* you may like to read the next adventures in *More Stories of Clever Polly and the Stupid Wolf.*

1. The Wolf at School

POLLY was on her way to school one morning, when she found the wolf trotting beside her. There were a great many other people around, so she was not particularly frightened, but she was curious.

'Where are you going, Wolf?' she asked.

'I'm going to school,' the wolf replied.

'My school?' Polly said.

'Of course, your school. Isn't it the best round here?' the wolf asked.

'Much the best. But Wolf ... if you're thinking you'll be able to get to eat me in school, you'll be disappointed. There are always crowds of us all together. If you tried to eat me, you'd get caught and probably shot. Or something.'

The wolf wasn't listening. 'Crowds? Of plump little girls? Of good, juicy little boys? Like this lot here?' he asked, looking round at the pavement covered with children hurrying towards the school gates.

'You won't have a chance to eat any of them,' Polly said, answering what she knew was in the wolf's mind.

'Hm. Pity. But I don't know why you are always thinking about food. That's not what I am going to school for. My mind is on higher things,' the wolf said virtuously.

'Higher than what?'

'Higher than my stomach. Brains, you stupid little girl. I am going to school to develop my brains. I am going to school so that I can become clever. Even cleverer than I am already,' the wolf added hastily.

'Who told you school would make you clever?' Polly asked.

'Read it in the paper. There was an advertisement. DO YOU WANT YOUR CHILD TO BE SMARTER THAN ANYONE ELSE'S? START EARLY LEARNING LESSONS NOW. I know you have lessons at school, and as I haven't got a child it seemed meant for me. I shall stay in your school until I can outsmart you, Miss Polly. Then, when I've eaten you up, and perhaps a dozen or so of these other children, I shan't need to learn any more and I shall leave.'

By now they had reached the school gates, and the other children were squeezing their way through. 'I don't think you can just walk in and join in the lessons without asking,' Polly said to the wolf, as they stood outside, left to the last.

'You must introduce me. Go on! If you're so clever, you can think of some way of getting me in. If you don't . . . Grrrrrr,' the wolf said, showing his teeth.

Polly looked round and saw that they were alone. 'All right. I'll try,' she said, and they went together across the playground to the cloakroom door.

'Good morning, Polly,' said Miss Wright, but when she saw Polly's companion, she said quickly, 'You know we don't allow pets in the classroom. Your dog must go home. Immediately!'

'He's not a dog. He's a friend who's come to stay with us from abroad. To learn English,' Polly said quickly, while she whispered to the wolf, 'Get up on your hind legs and try to look like a friend from abroad.' Beside her she could hear the wolf growling. 'Dog! Pet! Never been so insulted in my life!'

'He's very large. Isn't he too old for this class?' Miss Wright asked.

'He's big for his age,' Polly said.

'He's very dark. And hairy.'

'He's foreign. He doesn't speak the language very well yet. If he could sit next to me, I could

help him,' Polly said, thinking it would be better not to let the wolf sit next to Susie, who was the plumpest girl in the room, or next to Freddie, who might tease him into behaviour unbecoming to a pupil in Miss Wright's class.

'Foreign? How interesting. What country does he come from? What are you, dear?' Miss Wright asked the wolf. Polly wondered if he had ever been addressed as 'dear' before. His answer was indistinct, and Miss Wright looked puzzled for a moment, then she said, 'Hungary! Well now! I don't think we've ever had a child from Hungary in our school before. We must all do our best to make you feel at home.'

More Stories of Clever Polly and the Stupid Wolf is available in A Puffin Book.